J
Chapter
LABA
(red dot)
Oct u

SPYING
ON DRACULA

MARY LABATT

Kids Can Press acknowledges the financial support of the Ontario Arts Council, the Canada Council for the Arts and the Department of Cultural Heritage.

Published in Canada by
Kids Can Press Ltd.
29 Birch Avenue
Toronto, ON M4V 1E2

Published in the U.S. by
Kids Can Press Ltd.
85 River Rock Drive, Suite 202
Buffalo, NY 14207

Edited by Charis Wahl and Rivka Cranley
Designed by Marie Bartholomew
Typeset by Karen Birkemoe
Printed and bound in Canada

CM PA 99 0 9 8 7 6 5 4 3 2 1

Canadian Cataloguing in Publication Data

Labatt, Mary, 1944–
    Spying on Dracula

(Sam, dog detective)
ISBN 1-55074-634-0 (bound)   ISBN 1-55074-632-4 (pbk.)

I. Title. II. Series: Labatt, Mary, 1944– . Sam, dog detective.

PS8573.A135S69 1999   jC813'.54   C99-931529-3
PZ7.L1155 Sp 1999

Kids Can Press is a Nelvana company

To Larry,
with all my love

1. Sam Moves to Woodford

Sam glared out the back window of the car.

I hate the whole world, she fumed.

In the front seat, Joan and Bob chatted happily about their new house. Sam scowled at them. *Blah. Blah. Blah. I'm getting a big headache here, if anybody cares.*

Sam pressed her nose against the side window. Buildings zoomed by and trucks zipped past. *Every minute I'm getting farther from my friends. I'm going to hate Woodford.*

After a long time, the car stopped in front of a neat white house. Joan and Bob jumped out. "We're here, Sam!" they cried.

Sam turned her head away.

"Let's go, Sam," begged Joan. "Come and see our new house."

Sam scrunched her eyes shut.

Joan leaned into the car. "I said, we're here, Sam."

We are not here. You're here. I'm going back to the old neighborhood.

Bob muttered something to Joan. Then Sam felt a yank on her neck. Suddenly, she was dragged out of the car. *I don't believe this! First they sell my house and now they strangle me!*

"Sam!" shouted Joan. "Be a good dog!"

Sam glared. *I am a wonderful dog.* Throwing herself on the lawn, Sam screwed her eyes shut again and refused to budge. *This town has ten people in it. My life is wrecked, and it's your fault.*

Finally Joan and Bob went to look at their new house. Sam ignored them. She needed a new family.

As Sam lay there, a strange feeling crept over her. She felt as if she was being watched.

Next door, she saw a girl with a gentle face and long brown hair peeking from behind a curtain. The girl was about ten years old. Her soft brown eyes looked very, very sad.

Nosy kid, Sam growled.

From her bedroom window, Jennie Levinsky saw the enormous sheepdog refuse to get out of the car. But Jennie wasn't interested in dogs, especially huge hairy ones.

Yesterday, Jennie's best friend, Sarah, had moved away. Now this dog was going to live in Sarah's house. It wasn't fair. Jennie stomped out of her room, charged through the house and plopped down on the back steps.

All Jennie could think of was Sarah – their giggling fits, the sleepovers, the fort they'd made together. When Jennie looked at Sarah's house, she wanted to cry.

Jennie sat on the steps for a long time. She was thinking about the way Sarah told jokes, when she felt something watching her. Startled,

Jennie looked up. Staring at her from the next yard was the big sheepdog.

What's the matter with this dopey kid? Sam grumbled.

"Why is that dumb dog staring at me?" Jennie muttered.

The kid looks sad.

"That dog seems to be in a bad mood. But dogs don't have moods."

Kids have no reason to be sad. They have toys and birthdays and ice cream and candy and movies.

Just then, Joan called Sam from the back door. Jennie watched to see if the dog would answer.

Sam set her jaw firmly. *Let her call. I hate Woodford and I hate Joan.*

Sam sighed. *I wish I had a nice chocolate pudding with ketchup on it ... it might make me feel better.*

2. A Job for Jennie

Sam spent her first days in Woodford planning to run away. *I could hitchhike, but who'd pick up a dog? I'll have to walk and I'll get sore feet.*

Jennie spent the first days of summer wandering around her house. Every day was more boring than the last.

"We need to welcome our new neighbors. Maybe that will cheer you up, Jennie," said her dad at dinner one night.

Her mom agreed. "I brought them some ice cream from the store. You could take it over, Jennie."

The last thing Jennie wanted to do was talk to the people in Sarah's house. But after supper, she found herself knocking on Sarah's back door. A huge hairy face stared at her through the kitchen window.

When the door opened, a pretty blonde woman smiled and held the door wide open. "You're the little girl from next door, aren't you? Come in."

As soon as Jennie stepped through the door, her heart sank. Boxes were piled in Sarah's red and white kitchen. All the empty cupboards were open. Sarah was really gone.

"Let me introduce Sam," said the woman. The mountain of hair at the window glared.

The woman laughed. "She's cranky because she didn't want to move. She's being silly, of course. Moving to a new town doesn't matter to a dog."

Sam glared harder.

"Is Sam a girl?" asked Jennie.

"Yes. Her name is Samantha, but we call her Sam. And my name's Joan Kendrick. Please call me Joan."

"I'm Jennie Levinsky."

"Sam and I are pleased to know you, Jennie."

Speak for yourself. I'm not pleased to know anybody.

Jennie held out the tub of ice cream. "My parents sent you something from our store. It's our special ice cream. Everybody likes it."

"What kind of store do you have, Jennie?"

"Levinsky's Drugstore. My dad's the pharmacist and my mom runs the store. My brother Noel makes deliveries – he's thirteen. I'm going to get a job there when I'm older."

Sam sighed. *Boring.*

Joan poured some lemonade and they sat down. She was so friendly that Jennie told her about Sarah.

"Maybe you'd like to take Sam for a walk," suggested Joan. "We always pay someone to feed her and walk her while we're at work." She looked at Jennie closely. "Would you like to try it?"

Jennie eyed Sam nervously. "Are you sure she'll walk with me?"

"She's perfect. Sam loves walks."

"I guess I could," said Jennie slowly. "I'll ask my parents."

Sam looked back out the window and sighed. *Not that it matters. I'm running away soon.*

3. No Ordinary Dog

Jennie was back the next morning. "My parents like the idea of me walking Sam," she said.

"Wonderful!" said Joan. "I'll give you a key so you can get Sam while we're at work. All you have to do is feed her and walk her."

Jennie's face clouded.

"Don't worry," said Joan quickly. "It's easy." Joan took a box out of the cupboard. "Here's what Sam eats. One cup of kibble mixed with a can of liver dog food."

Sam sat down with a thud. *I never eat that junk! Tell her the truth, Joan. I don't touch that stuff.*

Sam gasped at Joan's next words. "Sam is a little fussy about dog food but don't worry about it."

Why should it worry her? It's me who's starving.

Joan looked firmly at Sam. "Sam has to eat dog food. She begs for junk food but it's not healthy."

Sam lay her head on her paws. *My life has hit bottom. Now we're going to have a big fuss about dog food.*

"Why not take her out now?" Joan suggested. "Sam will walk with you. She doesn't need a leash."

Sam peered at Jennie from under the table. *I happen to be a very intelligent dog. Leashes are for idiots ... and people.*

Jennie looked suspiciously at Sam's furry face. "Well ... I can try it."

When Joan opened the front door, Sam sprang to her feet, shoved through the door and raced down the walk. At the sidewalk, she turned and waited.

"That way," Jennie pointed.

Sam sailed down the street. She felt great to be outside, to be going somewhere. When she got to the corner, she stared at Jennie through the hair over her eyes.

"Sit down," Jennie commanded loudly.

Startled, Sam sat down. *No need to shout.*

Jennie tried not to look surprised. "Okay," she said sternly, "walk."

Sam sprang up and flounced across the road. *Why is this kid screaming orders? I'm not stupid.*

As they walked, Sam stopped at every corner. She didn't cross until Jennie told her she could. She pranced and strutted and poked into bushes. But she always waited for Jennie.

"This is easy!" Jennie laughed. "Sam, you're terrific."

Sam snorted. *Of course I'm terrific. Everyone knows that.* Sam looked carefully at Jennie. *Maybe you and I could have some fun. In my old neighborhood, I was a very well-known detective.*

While they waited at a corner, a car pulled up. Beth Morrison rolled down the window and waved at them. "Hi, Jennie! Did you get a dog?"

"Nope. She lives in Sarah's house."

"Bring her over!" yelled Beth as the car turned the corner.

"Okay!" shouted Jennie. "We'll come tomorrow!"

Hmm ... visiting is good. But I need some real excitement.

Later that night, Sam settled on the spare bed. She thought about Jennie. *Not a bad kid after all. Might be good for an adventure or two.* Sam sighed and let her mind wander over all her favorite things — giants and monsters, goblins and witches. She shivered deliciously. *I have to find an adventure,* she thought as she drifted off to sleep. *Boredom is bad.*

4. The Spookiest House in Town

I'M CRAZY ABOUT SPOOKY PLACES!

The next morning, Jennie knocked on Sam's door. Sam's head shot out as soon as the door opened. Joan was still in her bathrobe, looking sleepy and surprised.

"I came early so I could show Sam the town," explained Jennie.

Sam shoved past Jennie and dashed down the walk. *This should take about five minutes.*

Itching to be off, Sam stepped from foot to foot. *Let's go, kid. Woodford awaits.*

"See you later, Joan," called Jennie as she hurried after Sam.

When Jennie caught up, Sam eyed her with interest. *Now show me the exciting stuff. There has to be a mystery somewhere in this crummy town.*

"I don't know what to show you first, Sam," Jennie said. "Maybe we should go to Main Street."

It's a start.

All morning, Jennie and Sam poked up and down the streets of Woodford. It was a peaceful town nestled in rolling farmland. Only the main street was busy.

When they got to the drugstore, Jennie looked in the window. Her father was talking on the telephone at the back of the store. He waved.

"We'll come back when he's not busy, Sam," said Jennie. "We have all summer."

They walked through the schoolyard to Jennie's old classroom. Sam put her front paws on the windowsill and yawned. *Boring.*

"There's nothing to see here," said Jennie, peering at the jumbled desks and chairs. She looked down at Sam. "Hey, I know. I'll show you the spookiest house in Woodford."

Sam's heart soared. *Yes!* She whirled around.

Let's go! I'm crazy about spooky places.

Jennie led Sam past their houses toward a small side street on the edge of town. Across the street, inside a sagging wire fence, stood a row of tall pine trees.

Jennie and Sam crossed the road and walked along the fence until Jennie found an opening in the underbrush. Kneeling down, she peeked through. "This is the creepiest place you'll ever see, Sam."

Sam looked at the old house behind the trees. Dark snaked over stone walls and windows. A thick silence hung over the dim yard. *Perfect!* she chuckled happily.

Jennie shivered. "Some weird guy named McIver lives here. Nobody sees him and nobody ever comes to visit."

Sam peered through the underbrush again. *I bet this house has ghosts. That's why nobody comes.*

"Noel says McIver doesn't even answer the door on Halloween. Sarah and I were too scared to come here."

Sam chortled. *Ghosts would be roaring around on Halloween.*

"We think he's a criminal. This old house would be a great hideout."

They stared at the gloomy house. No sunlight filtered through the trees. Sam sniffed. It smelled musty, like a place that had been forgotten.

"Noel says McIver hardly ever turns on lights – even at night."

Hmm … maybe he's a goblin. I heard goblins can see in the dark.

"But Noel says he sometimes sees a small light moving around in there."

Maybe McIver's from outer space. Maybe the light's from a spaceship.

"Maybe he keeps the lights off so the police think the house is empty."

Maybe he's been dead for years. I think he's a ghost.

"You know what else Noel told me?"

The hair over Sam's eyes lifted with interest.

"When Noel delivers something from the store, McIver won't let him in. He shouts through the door to leave the package on the porch."

Aha! He doesn't want anybody to see him. Sam's head buzzed joyfully. *That means he's hiding something ... And if he's hiding something, that means there's a mystery ... And where there's a mystery, there's excitement ...*

"Let's go, Sam," said Jennie. "I hate this place."

I love it! Sam poked her nose through the underbrush and listened.

"Come on, Sam," urged Jennie. "Criminals don't like to be stared at. Even by a dog."

Sam didn't move. A tiny sound was coming from the house, a sound so faint that only Sam could hear it. Click ... Click ... Click ...

Sam cocked her head. Click ... Click ...

Jennie tugged at Sam's collar. "Let's go, Sam!"

Sam didn't budge. The clicking stopped. An eerie silence hung over the yard.

Suddenly Jennie put her arm around Sam and whispered, "Sam, there's something right over our heads!"

A bat hung from a branch above them. Its papery wings were folded over its back. Just as Jennie and Sam looked up, its bulging eyes opened, blinked and closed.

"Bats get tangled in your hair!" Jennie covered her hair with her hands.

Big deal. Sam looked back at the house and listened again. *I'm busy.*

Jennie couldn't take her eyes off the bat. "Move slowly. Maybe we can sneak away."

Don't bother me. Sam's eyes were fixed on the house.

Jennie slowly backed away from the fence, her eyes glued to the bat. Finally Sam followed.

As soon as they were clear of the trees, Jennie began to run. She and Sam raced to the open field behind McIver's house and fell on the grass.

"I hate bats," Jennie shuddered.

Sam wasn't listening. She was looking back at the house. *Very interesting. Hmm …*

Jennie stood up. "Let's go and see Beth. I don't want to stay here." She started toward town. "Come on, Sam."

All Sam's fury about Woodford was forgotten. Her mind whirled happily at the thought of a mystery. Humming a little tune to herself, she followed Jennie across the field. Her long fur floated around her as she walked.

Ghosts would be good. Ghosts would be very good.

5. Beth Gets Curious

Sam was still humming as she followed Jennie through the quiet streets. *It's a good thing I'm a detective. I'll have this thing figured out in no time.*

When Jennie knocked on Beth's door, it banged open. A small boy with bright red hair shouted, "Come in!" Another boy exactly the same popped up behind him and grinned.

Pushing past Jennie, the twins raced through the door and pounced on Sam. Sam sat down and slurped at their faces. The boys squealed and shrieked.

Beth's mother came around the corner of the house carrying plants. "Jennie," she smiled, "it's nice to see you. How have you been?"

"Fine thanks, Mrs. Morrison. Is Beth home?"

"She sure is. She's moaning about having nothing to do this summer. Come on in."

Jennie followed Beth's mother into the sunny kitchen. Mrs. Morrison poured some milk and opened a box of doughnuts. "Help yourself, Jennie."

Sam and the twins piled into the house. One of them grabbed a jelly doughnut and passed it to Sam. She dove under the table, gulped it down and smacked her chops. *Terrific.* She nudged both boys with her round black nose. *Keep it up, you guys.*

When Beth came downstairs, Sam watched from under the table. Beth was small and skinny and had the same fluffy red hair as her little brothers.

Sam popped out from under the table, marched over to Beth and lifted her paw. "Pleased to meet you," laughed Beth as they shook hands.

"This is Sam," said Jennie. "I've got a job walking her."

"Wow!" Beth looked at Sam's huge furry face. "She's nice, Jennie."

I'm a lot better than nice. You'll see.

Beth and Jennie went out to sit on the porch.

"What are you doing this summer, Jennie?" asked Beth.

"Nothing much. Just my job with Sam."

"I don't have anything to do either." Beth paused. "Maybe I could come with you and Sam sometimes."

"Sure," Jennie smiled.

Just then, Sam staggered out to the porch and flopped down with a thud. *I'm sick.* She lay her head on her paws. The world was spinning, and a woozy feeling was growing in her stomach. *I think I'm getting the flu. It couldn't be the doughnuts. Good food never hurt anybody.*

"Sam looks tired," said Beth. "Where did you take her this morning?"

"We went up Main Street and over to the school." Jennie leaned back in the swing. "And I showed Sam the old McIver place."

"How close did you get?"

"We looked through the trees."

"It's creepy, isn't it?"

Jennie twirled a piece of her long hair. "It sure is. We saw a bat."

"I thought bats lived in caves."

"Well, we saw one in McIver's trees, and it blinked at me in a very sickening way."

"How come nobody ever sees McIver?" asked Beth.

Jennie shrugged.

"Do you ever wonder why there are hardly ever any lights on?" Beth looked thoughtful. "I'd love to know what he does in there."

You're lucky you met me then, because I'm going to find out. Sam burped. *That is, if I live. I seem to be getting a weak stomach.*

6. Jennie's Gift

Sam woke up the next morning feeling fine. *Must have been the 24-hour flu. I wonder where I could get some sardines and chocolate bars for breakfast.*

Next door, Jennie decided to take Sam for a picnic. She quickly packed a lunch and went to get Sam.

Joan smiled as Sam wedged herself in the doorway.

I love picnics. Let's go.

Sam galloped down the walk and turned toward the woods. Jennie ran after her, the picnic bag flapping against her legs, and her brown hair streaming behind her.

When they got to the edge of town, they headed for the field behind the McIver house. The tall pines swayed in the summer breeze.

Sam nosed over to McIver's fence and listened. *I need to find out what he's doing.*

"Come on, Sam," called Jennie. "Forget McIver."

Not a chance. After the picnic I'm coming back.

Through the warm fields of early summer they raced, until Sam spotted the perfect picnic place. She lay down on a flat rock beside a creek. *So ... what's for lunch? Unpack the food.*

Jennie sat cross-legged in the grass. She propped the bag between her knees, and pulled out two jam sandwiches, a can of orange pop, two apples and a bag of chocolate chip cookies. She divided the food into two piles.

Sam chortled happily. *Glad you didn't listen to the dog-food speech, kid.*

"The orange pop is for me, Sam," said Jennie. "Pop will give you worms. You can drink out of the creek."

Sam gasped. *Me? Drink slimy water? It's full of oozy plants and dirty, creepy frogs. I love orange pop.*

Jennie was munching on her sandwich when the sound rang inside her head. It was like a thought, but Jennie hadn't thought it. It seemed to echo from far away. 'Me? Drink slimy water? It's full of oozy plants and dirty, creepy frogs.' Jennie stopped in mid-bite.

Sam stared at Jennie. *Fish make their messes in that water.*

The echoing voice sounded inside Jennie's head again. She dropped her sandwich. "Fish make their messes in that water?" she muttered.

Why should I drink fish mess? You don't!

Jennie clapped her hands over her ears. She had heard 'Why should I drink fish mess? You don't!' She gaped at Sam.

The hair over Sam's eyes lifted. *Fish mess has germs in it. I could get a horrible disease.*

Holding her head, Jennie groaned. Inside her

head she heard, 'Fish mess has germs in it. I could get a horrible disease.'

"I don't want anybody to get a disease!" Jennie cried, looking around wildly. "Who thinks I want them to get sick?" She squinted at the woods, the grass and the sky.

Sam just stared.

"Sam, someone is talking to me!" whispered Jennie. "Someone's saying stupid stuff about fish mess and oozy plants and horrible diseases." Jennie stood up and peered around. "Someone must be hiding in those trees."

Sam sighed. *Why are people so thick-headed? Of course someone is talking to you!*

Jennie shrieked as the echo sounded inside her head. "There it goes again!" she yelled, shaking her head as if she could shake the sound out.

Sam chortled. *It's me! I'm talking to you.*

Jennie looked at the woods. "Who's there?" she yelled at the trees. "Who said that?"

Sam chuckled. *I did, Jennie. Me. Right in front of you.*

Jennie covered her ears. "I can't stand

this!" she screamed.

It's me, Jennie.

"Who's me?" yelled Jennie. "Sam, someone is torturing me!"

It's me. Sam. I'm talking to you.

"What did you say?" she asked in a small voice.

Sam stared at Jennie. *I said, I'm the one talking to you.*

Jennie squirmed and looked over her shoulder. "I must be nuts asking a dog what she said."

Sam stared harder.

Jennie gawked at Sam. "Is it really you?"

I can't tell you a million times. It's me talking. And I am not drinking water with fish mess in it. Sam sniffed. *Frogs mess in it, too, so it's really disgusting.*

Jennie's brown eyes widened in shock.

Sam blinked. There was no sound, except the buzz of tiny insects in the grass.

"All right!" exploded Jennie. "Have the pop!" She poured some pop on a plastic bag. Sam slurped noisily, licked the bag and smacked her chops. Then she nibbled daintily at her sandwich.

"How did I know you wanted the pop, Sam?"

Sam calmly looked up from her sandwich. *I told you.*

"I must have thought it," Jennie muttered.

Sam chewed slowly. *I'm the one who thought it. You heard it.*

"I didn't hear it. How could I hear it?"

You heard it, all right.

Jennie jumped up. "What did you say?"

You heard me.

"This isn't happening!"

Sam polished off her apple and belched. *Of course it's happening.*

"I can hear your thoughts!" exclaimed Jennie.

I thought you'd be able to. Most dogs are too stupid to notice when someone has this special gift. Very few people have it, and I can always tell. Sam licked cookie crumbs contentedly. *I don't know if I've told you this, but I'm no ordinary dog.*

Groaning, Jennie sank back in the grass. Nobody would believe this.

Let's go and look at that creepy house. I'm a famous detective and I smell a mystery.

Jennie sat bolt upright. "I heard that! You want to go and look at McIver's place! You think you're a detective."

Sam yawned and licked her big black nose with her pink tongue. *I don't just think I'm a detective. I am a detective. I want to know what McIver's doing in there. I heard a funny clicking sound.*

"A clicking sound?"

Yup.

"What could that be?"

I'm going to find out. Sam lumbered to her feet. *Let's go.*

"It's dangerous, Sam," said Jennie nervously. "Criminals aren't thrilled when people spy on them."

Phooey. If it gets dangerous, I'll bite him. Come on.

"Would you really bite someone?"

Of course. I've got wonderful teeth. Sam started toward McIver's. *Coming?*

Slowly, Jennie got to her feet. She packed up the picnic things and followed Sam to McIver's fence. "I can't believe I'm talking to a dog," she muttered.

Sam poked her head through an opening in the underbrush and listened. Suddenly, the hair on the back of her neck prickled and a low growl rumbled in her throat.

"What is it?" whispered Jennie. "What's the matter?"

Listen! Sam craned her neck to get a better look.

Then Jennie heard it. Ghostly moaning floated through the yard. She couldn't tell where it came from, but it was a dreadful sound, mournful and strange.

Ghosts! Crooks don't moan. Sam looked over at Jennie. *The place is haunted!*

Jennie turned pale.

How could you live so close to a mystery and ignore it?

"I told you. We were too scared to come here."

Hmph! That ghost will be sorry I moved to Woodford.

7. The Detectives Get to Work

At Beth's house, Sam flopped down beside the porch swing. Jennie and Beth were talking about McIver — the clicking sound, hardly any lights, the bat, the moaning and how nobody ever saw him.

Beth started to chew a fingernail. "Let's find out what makes McIver so weird."

Sam looked up. *Yeah. We'll find out his secret and get our picture in the paper. We'll be famous.*

Jennie looked doubtful. "We'd have to stand at his fence every day. That could be dangerous."

"We'd be careful," said Beth. She stood up and paced. "And we'll take Sam. She can protect us."

"That's what she said."

"Who said?"

"Uh ... nobody. I mean – uh – never mind." Sam chuckled.

Beth snapped her fingers. "I've got an idea. Be right back."

Sam sidled over to Beth's little brothers, who were having a snack. She sniffed their plates and gobbled a piece of banana cake.

Jennie shook her head. "Sam, I don't think cake is good for you."

Sam kept eating. *Of course it's good for me.* She came back to the swing and grabbed a mouthful of potato chips from Beth's bowl.

"You're going to get sick," Jennie whispered.

Shut up, said Sam as she crunched down the rest of the chips.

Jennie gasped. "Don't tell me to shut up!"

Just then, Beth appeared with some pencils and paper.

"Jennie, you just talked to the dog!"

Jennie squirmed. "Uh ... I didn't exactly talk to her."

"You did. You told her not to tell you to shut up."

"Yeah … Well … She … I … Forget it." Jennie glowered at Sam.

Sam yawned.

Beth looked at Sam. Then she looked back at Jennie. "You were talking to Sam. I heard you."

Jennie blushed. "It sounds crazy."

"What sounds crazy?" Beth's green eyes bored into Jennie.

"Uh … Something strange happened to me today."

"What happened?" Beth leaned forward. Her small body tensed. "Tell me."

Jennie shrugged. "Well … I … I hear what Sam is thinking."

Beth's face clouded. "You can hear what a dog is thinking?"

"It's strange. It rings in my head like a thought." Jennie clasped her hands nervously. "Only it's Sam's thought, not mine."

Beth ran her fingers through her fluffy red hair. "You're right. That is really strange."

Believe it, Beth. It's the truth.

"Why would she believe it, Sam? It's too weird!" Jennie exclaimed.

"You did it again!" cried Beth. "You just talked to the dog!"

"I know," groaned Jennie. "She just said, 'Believe it, Beth.'"

"Oh."

"I mean she didn't actually say it. She thought it."

"Sure." Beth looked stunned.

Jennie's face turned bright red. Sam chuckled.

Once Beth got over the shock, she asked a million questions. She loved the idea of Sam being a detective. "Will Sam talk to me?" she asked hopefully.

Jennie hugged Sam. "Say something to Beth, Sam."

Can't. The hair over Sam's eyes moved up and down.

"What do you mean you can't?"

I can only talk to someone who has the special gift. Sam held her head proudly. *It takes an extremely clever dog to know when someone's got it.*

Jennie turned to Beth. "Sam says she can only talk to someone who has a special gift."

"Oh," said Beth, disappointed. She looked at her new friends as if they were very, very weird.

Later that morning, Sam watched suspiciously as Beth pulled out her paper and pencils. *I hope Beth isn't one of these kids that likes writing.*

Beth arranged her pencils neatly. "We need a plan. Let's make a list of the things real detectives do."

She sat on the ground and wrote on the top of the page: How to Investigate a Mystery. She tapped her pencil. "Think, Jennie. How do they do it on TV?"

"Well, mostly they just follow people around."

Beth wrote: 1. Follow him wherever he goes.

Jennie thought for a minute. "Only he never goes anywhere."

Sam stretched out and yawned. *That's why we're interested in him, you nitwits.*

"We'll put it down anyway," said Beth.

Sam sighed. *Humans waste all their time writing.*

Jennie and Beth tried to remember all the detective shows they'd seen. Soon they had a list of six things. Beth read them aloud.

How to Investigate a Mystery
1. Follow him wherever he goes.
2. Hide in the bushes and watch his house.
3. Look in his windows.
4. Spy around his property.
5. Talk to somebody who knows him.
6. Interview him.

Suddenly, Sam got up and started to pace. *I'm sick of all this writing! Let's get started.*

"Sam wants to get started," said Jennie.

"Maybe we could take her for a walk."

Yeah. Quit wasting time. Let's go.

Beth and Jennie followed Sam. When they got to the field, it started to rain.

They tiptoed to McIver's house from the field and crouched in the weeds. Blank windows stared back at them. There was nothing to see. And nothing to hear, except the sound of water dripping from the trees.

Suddenly Sam cocked her head. *I hear something!*

Jennie nudged Beth. "Sam says she hears something!"

The girls strained to listen. After a few minutes, they heard rumbling, and a truck turned into McIver's driveway. The truck lumbered up the rutted lane and stopped beside the house. Two men got out and looked around.

"You sure this is the place?" asked the driver.

"Yup." The other man opened the back of the truck. "Let's get this thing out of here."

The driver picked his way through the mud and went up McIver's rickety steps. The girls couldn't see the front door, and they could hear only muffled voices.

"I wish we could hear what they're saying," whispered Jennie.

Sam glanced at her scornfully. *Humans are so deaf!*

They watched as the men went back to the truck and lifted out a long wooden box.

"What did they say, Sam?" asked Jennie.

McIver wants them to leave it on the porch.

Jennie poked Beth. "Sam says McIver wants it left on the porch. That's what he always says to Noel!"

"I wonder why he won't let anyone in."

Because he's got a secret! Sam shivered with happiness. *Wonderful.*

8. One Rainy Night

TIME FOR ACTION!

Jennie and Beth decided to take Sam for a walk after supper. When they knocked on Sam's front door, the rain had slowed to a drizzle.

Joan said Sam had been sitting beside the door. "I can't understand it," she said. "It's as if she knew you were coming."

Sam stared impatiently at the girls.

"It's going to be a dark night," said Jennie nervously when they got outside.

Beth pulled a small flashlight out of her raincoat pocket. "I brought this. But I'll keep it turned off until we need it."

In the murky twilight, they circled through the field behind McIver's house. When they got to the old orchard on the far side, they squatted in the wet weeds.

Long shadows crept over the house. The vines were like snakes against the stone walls.

"I – I'm scared." Jennie's voice shook.

"This is a very spooky place." Beth sounded nervous but determined. She chewed fiercely on a fingernail.

Relax. I'm the toughest dog in town.

"We should wait until it's really dark before we climb the fence," said Beth sensibly.

Sam bumped Jennie with her nose. *Hey, what about me? I can't climb fences.*

Jennie tugged on Beth's arm. "Sam can't climb the fence."

They thought for a moment. The darkness deepened around them. The silence of the old house reached out for them.

Sam nudged Jennie. *I've got it!*

Jennie's face lit up. "I've got it!" she whispered. "Here's what Sam can do."

Beth listened carefully.

"Sam can go to McIver's driveway," Jennie

explained. "She'll wander down the lane and sniff a few bushes. McIver won't notice a dog. We'll climb the fence and meet her in the back yard."

Beth grinned. "Perfect plan," she said. "Nobody would think a dog was spying."

Sam snorted. *Of course it's perfect. I thought of it.*

When Sam got to McIver's lane, she turned into the pitch black yard.

At the rear of the house, a yellow light was moving in a window.

Slowly, silently, Sam crept around the back of the house. Crack! A twig snapped underfoot. She froze.

Nothing happened.

Through the blackness, Sam sniffed her way to the girls. Thump! Thump! The girls jumped off the fence.

A little silence would be good.

Beth pulled on Jennie's sleeve. "I just thought of something." Her small body was tense. "Sam could get trapped here. We need an escape hole in case McIver comes out and she can't get past him."

Smart kid. Sam nosed toward the fence and sniffed up and down. She stopped.

"S-Sam's found a hole," squeaked Jennie.

They edged over to Sam. Beth quickly shone her flashlight. There was a gaping hole that Sam could crawl through.

Time for action.

Jennie's chest was tight with fear. They had to be careful.

Sam sighed. *Come on. We're here for detective work. Remember?*

She wedged herself between the girls. *Quit stalling. We came to spy, not stand around.*

"S-Sam wants us to get going," Jennie whispered.

Beth drew herself up bravely. "Sam's right. Let's do it."

Jennie and Beth got down on their hands and

knees. Hearts thumping, they crawled toward the flickering light.

When they were beneath the window, the girls stood up. The window was too high!

Beth tugged on Jennie's arm and pointed to an old wooden bench. Creeping like silent shadows, they picked up the bench and put it under the window. Holding on to each other, they climbed onto the bench and crouched down.

Slowly, they stood up, but Beth was still too short to see over the windowsill.

Sam watched from the darkness. *Come on, Jennie. You're the only one who's tall enough to see.*

Jennie straightened up until her eyes were almost level with the windowsill. She held her breath and stretched her head a bit more …

9. What Jennie Saw

Jennie's legs turned to jelly. In front of her was the strangest thing she had ever seen!

A wild-haired creature was leaning over a table. Its nose and mouth were one long black tube. On the table sat the wooden box the men had delivered that afternoon. The creature was doing something inside it. A beam of light streamed from its tube-like mouth into the box.

All around the room were fantastic machines. A jumble of tools, bits of wire and little pieces of equipment sat on sagging shelves. Jennie's eyes swept over electronic circuit boards, keyboards and computer screens. The room looked like a spaceship.

The creature loomed over the box. While it worked, it cocked its head slightly as if it was listening to something inside the box. Wherever the creature turned its head, the light from its long mouth shone in that direction.

All around the creature's head floated a wispy halo of dark hair. Its body was greenish. It looked like something that had crawled out of a swamp. Or another world.

Jennie was frozen with fear. She couldn't take her eyes off the strange thing in front of her.

The creature stretched. The light from its mouth circled the gloomy room. Then the light looked straight at Jennie. She was trapped in its beam. There was no escape!

The creature reached up and shut off its light. For a moment, Jennie felt blind. Then she could see its face. It stared at her, its two pale eyes bulging like the huge eyes of a grasshopper.

Jennie's whole body tingled with terror.

With a squeal, Jennie grabbed Beth, tumbled backward off the bench, and gasped, "Quick! Run! Run for your life!"

Through the night they stumbled. Jennie staggered over the lumpy ground, fell and twisted her ankle. But she couldn't stop. Behind her, she could feel the thing breathing down on her neck. She had to get to the road.

Beth ran straight into a prickly bush and thrashed wildly to get out. Her arms stung and her face was scratched. She fell, scrambled to her feet and kept running. Then she glimpsed headlights flashing behind the pine trees. The road! She had to make it.

Sam stayed in the back yard for a few minutes to see if McIver was coming. *There's a vicious dog here, McIver.* Sam bared her fangs and snarled. *We'll have a huge battle,* she thought savagely. *This is great!*

Jennie heard snarling through the darkness. Frantically she looked behind her. No Beth. No Sam. Maybe the creature had them!

Jennie risked another quick glance back, terrified that she would look straight into those pale bulging eyes. But she saw only the outline of the dark house.

Another growl came out of the night, and Jennie caught a flash of white darting through the trees. "Sam!" she hissed. "I'm over here."

Stay where you are, panted Sam.

Jennie could vaguely see a small shape lurching across the yard. It must be Beth.

Then Sam was beside her. *Some fun, huh?*

Jennie's heart was pounding too loudly for her to hear. "W-where's Beth?"

She's coming.

Thump. Thump. Jennie could hear the sound of footsteps. "H-hurry, Beth!"

Beth grabbed on to Jennie, puffing and panting. "Let's get out of here!" she wheezed.

Just then, something swooped down at them with a squeaking noise. They ducked. A second later, it swooshed back over their heads. The bat!

Jennie shrieked. Sam snapped at the air. Beth waved her arms wildly.

Half dragging, half carrying each other, the girls dashed toward the road. The bat swooped and soared above them.

"W-we've got to get to that streetlight," gasped Jennie. "B-bats don't like light."

If it comes any closer, I'll chomp it to bits.

When the girls got across the road, they threw themselves down under the light. Giddy with relief, they watched the bat disappear into the darkness.

Gradually their hearts slowed, and their chests stopped hurting. Then they looked at each other. Jennie's knees were scraped and her hair hung in long dirty strands. Beth was covered with mud, and her face and arms were a mass of ugly scratches. Prickly branches and sticks hung from her curls. Only Sam looked fine – a little muddy, but fine.

Beth yanked at the sticks in her tangled hair. "I'll never get these things out!"

Jennie squinted at the dark line of trees. "I – I want to go home." Tears stung her eyes.

Beth hopped up. "Let's go then." She took Jennie's arm, and together they limped down the road. "We're safe now, Jennie."

Sam followed behind, humming happily to

herself. *Now* this *is what I call a good time.*

When they got to Jennie's house, Beth said, "Don't forget, we're meeting in Sam's back yard tomorrow at ten."

"All right," Jennie sniffled.

Later that night, Sam settled down on the living room sofa. She sighed with happiness. *Just what I needed. A little excitement.*

Suddenly she sat bolt upright. *Hey! I wonder what Jennie saw? In all the confusion, I forgot to ask.* Sam lay back down. *I hope it was something good — like a monster with five heads.*

10. Quitters Are Wimps

At ten o'clock the next morning, Jennie was still nervous. Everywhere she looked she saw weird eyes and creatures with long tube mouths.

Sam nudged Jennie. *So ... what did you see? I'm getting old here waiting for you to tell me.*

Just then Beth appeared. Sam snuffled in Beth's bag, found a humbug and crunched noisily. *Hurry up. Tell us.*

Beth looked at Jennie's pale face. "Did you get in trouble?"

Jennie shook her head. "My parents were at the store, and Noel never notices anything."

Beth sat down. "Nobody saw me either. I went straight to the shower."

Never mind that. Get to the good stuff.

"What did you see when you looked in the window?" Beth asked.

Sam was getting cranky. *We're waiting.*

Jennie was startled. "You mean I didn't tell you?"

"No. I just ran because you ran."

I'm sick of this stalling.

Jennie took a deep breath. "I saw an enormous green creature doing something inside that long big box."

Beth stiffened. "What did it look like?"

"It had crazy hair, and its mouth and nose stuck out like a black tube. Some kind of a light shone out of its mouth …" Jennie paused. "But the worst thing was its eyes … Its eyes were terrible …" She looked frightened. "Beth, that thing looked right at me."

"Looked at you?" Beth started to chew a fingernail.

Jennie nodded slowly.

"A light shone out of a tube mouth?"

Jennie nodded again.

"It was green?"

"Yeah. Except for its face."

Hmm ... a monster would be good.

"If it saw you, it knows about us!" Beth looked fearfully around the yard as if she expected to see a green hulk staggering across the grass.

Jennie chewed her lip unhappily.

Quit worrying. I've got great teeth.

Beth gulped. "What were its eyes like?"

Jennie twirled a strand of hair. When she spoke, she stammered a little. "W-well ... they were round and bulging like a bug's eyes. Th-there was sort of goggles or something over them."

"Bulging? Like a praying mantis?" Beth stood up and started to pace.

Insect eyes, huh?

Jennie nodded.

"And a mouth that stuck out like a tube?" Beth was thinking hard.

Jennie nodded again.

Sam whirled around in delight. *McIver's a big*

insect! Some experiment made him grow. Now he hides in Woodford and pretends he's a person.

Jennie's eyes widened. "Sam says he's an insect. She thinks some experiment made him grow to the size of a human."

Beth paced back and forth and chomped on her nails again. "That would explain why he won't open the door."

Yeah. If he opens the door, everybody will know he's a bug.

Beth furrowed her brow. "How could a light shine out of his mouth?"

Jennie shrugged.

Maybe he's an alien insect. Lights shine out of aliens all the time.

"Sam's talking about alien insects."

"How many arms and legs did he have?" probed Beth, her small face scrunched up with curiosity.

"I only saw two arms. I couldn't see his legs."

"He has bug eyes, but he has two arms — like a person," puzzled Beth.

Sam trotted back and forth happily. *Aha!*

Definitely part bug, part alien.

"Sam may be right," Jennie considered. "He could be from another planet."

Sam suddenly stopped pacing. *What about that moaning?*

"I don't know what the moaning was. Maybe he is a ghost after all," said Jennie. "His eyes were really pale."

"He can't be a ghost. Ghosts are white, not green," objected Beth. "Maybe he's a mutant —" She stopped and her body went rigid. "I wonder what that box is for?"

I bet he's making a new monster. He probably had parts delivered.

Jennie gasped. "Creating a monster! In the box!"

"Uh-oh." Beth stopped. "Like Frankenstein?" Her green eyes blazed with excitement.

Sam's mind whirred. *Don't forget that moaning. Maybe he's some kind of alien ghost. Maybe that's why his eyes look dead ... Maybe he is dead. Maybe dead people moan ... What about half-bug aliens? They probably moan all the time.*

"Sam's talking about the moaning again," said Jennie.

"We'd better write down the clues." Beth reached for her bag. "That's the only way we'll remember everything."

Don't start writing! Sam groaned. *I hate writing.*

Beth pulled pencils and paper out of her bag. "Think of clues," she said firmly.

Beth wrote furiously. Sam listened as she read out the clues.

Hardly ever turns on the lights at night.
Sometimes a small light moves inside.
Doesn't answer the door.
Moaning sound.
Doesn't have any friends.
Big box delivered.
Light comes out of its mouth.
Clicking sound.
Bat in the trees.
Didn't chase us.
Long tube mouth.
Pale bulging dead bug eyes.

"Now we need another list of all the things these clues could mean," said Beth.

Sam groaned again. *Why don't we just go over there and look around? No decent detective solves anything with a list!*

The girls tried to figure out what the clues meant, but nothing worked. They couldn't see what clicking, moaning and bats had to do with pale buggy eyes.

"This is useless!" cried Beth in frustration.

Of course it's useless. I could have saved you all that stupid writing. Sam looked at Jennie haughtily. *If anybody listened.*

"I hate lists!" Beth threw down her pencil and ripped the paper into little bits. "What kind of creature is it anyway?"

"Maybe we should forget about it," suggested Jennie timidly.

Beth gritted her teeth. "No way." Two red spots burned on her cheeks. "I'm going to find out what it is."

Me too. Quitters are wimps.

"Don't call me a wimp, Sam." Jennie sounded hurt. "I saw it. If you had seen it, you'd be scared, too."

Phooey. I'd never be scared of a big bug.

"Its eyes are creepy, Sam. Remember the bat's eyes, how they bulged in that sickening way? McIver's eyes are like that."

Sam sat bolt upright. *Like the bat's eyes?*

"Yeah." Jennie shook her head. "It is definitely not a human being."

Hmmmm . . . Interesting.

"What are you thinking, Sam?" Jennie asked.

Well . . . If the bat hangs around his house and if he has eyes like the bat . . . What does that tell you?

Jennie turned to Beth. "What does it mean if McIver has eyes like the bat?"

Beth shrugged. "Maybe he's related to the bat." She stopped and clenched her fists with excitement. "Maybe he's part bat, not part bug!"

"Part bat?" Jennie gasped.

Excitement raced deliciously up and down Sam's spine as she pictured hideous, silent bats. In her mind, the bats had human faces and blinked at her as they flew past.

A bat person. Sam hummed cheerily. *Now that has a nice ring to it.*

11. Dracula

Sam told Jennie about a TV show Joan and Bob had watched. It was about some guy named Count Dracula who turned into a bat.

When Jennie told Beth, Beth screeched. "I have that comic at home! Wait a minute." She ran out of the yard.

"This tells all about Dracula," Beth panted when she got back. They raced up to Jennie's room and shut the door.

I hate reading, muttered Sam, and hopped up on Jennie's bed. She glared at the girls as they spread the comic on the floor. *Is this your idea of a good time?*

"It's research, Sam," explained Jennie. "We

need to know about Dracula."

Hmph. Sam fixed her eyes on Jennie. *You don't happen to have any pickles, do you? I need a peanut butter and pickle sandwich with ketchup.*

"Yuck," groaned Jennie. "That'll make you sick. You should eat dog biscuits."

Sam squinted fiercely at Jennie. *I want a sandwich with pickles, peanut butter and ketchup.* She stretched out on the bed. *It's delicious. I ate one at a picnic when I was a puppy.*

Beth was flipping through the comic. "Let her eat whatever she wants. Otherwise she'll bug us while we read."

Sam lifted her head. *See what a lovely kid Beth is?*

Jennie sighed. "Maybe you're right, Beth. I can't spend my life fighting about food. Be right back."

When Jennie came back with the sandwich, Sam gobbled it up and belched. *Hurry up and get this reading done. I'm bored.*

The girls huddled over the comic. "There are bats in Transylvania that turn into people!" cried Beth. "I knew it!"

Jennie was looking at the next page. "Dracula lived in Transylvania."

Beth turned the page. "This says he turned into a bat whenever he wanted!"

"Yeah. And all the people in the village were scared of him." Jennie pointed to a picture of terrified villagers.

"'He went out every night looking for victims,'" read Beth.

"Look at this." Jennie pointed. "He lived in an old castle and slept all day in a coffin."

"Look at this part!" cried Beth. "He had long fangs so he could bite people."

Sam was no longer bored. *Dracula, huh?* She closed her eyes and played a scene in her mind. Perched on the edge of a wild cliff was a spooky castle. Out of a window flew a black bat. In midair he changed into a person. Dracula! His lips pulled back to reveal huge fangs.

"Dracula terrorized Transylvania for a long time. Then he disappeared," read Jennie. She looked at Beth with wide brown eyes. "They never found him."

Sam's head whipped up. *Aha! This gets better and better.*

Beth's red hair seemed to stand on end. "I bet we know where he is."

Sam chortled happily as she jumped up and down. *What a lovely little town this is!*

"Look." Beth pointed to a picture of a hideous bat.

Jennie's voice squeaked. "A-are you thinking what I'm thinking?"

Beth nodded. "I think the bat that flew over us was Dracula."

"And the bat Sam and I saw in the trees?"

"I think that was him too."

The color drained from Jennie's face. "You think he was watching us?"

Beth nodded.

If we've got Dracula right here in Woodford, let's capture him! We can sell him to a zoo.

Jennie gasped. "We are not going to capture Dracula, Sam."

"Sam wants to capture him?"

"Yeah. And sell him to a zoo."

Beth scrunched up her face and thought hard. "What about that big box?"

"Yeah." Jennie did not want to voice the terrible thought that had crept into her mind.

Beth leaned forward. "What if that box is his coffin?"

"D-d-do you think he was making a bed in it when I saw him?" squeaked Jennie.

Beth gulped. "Yup."

Of course it's his coffin! Of course he was making his bed. Why didn't I think of that? Delightedly, Sam danced on the bed and whipped the bedspread into little mounds.

But all Jennie could think of was the dark, wild creature she saw hovering over the coffin.

That night Sam tried to relax with Joan and Bob, but she couldn't. *What's Dracula doing? I have to know.* She stood up, turned around and tried to get comfortable. In seconds she was up again. *Maybe I should go to his house.*

She flopped down on the hard floor. *It's dangerous, though ... Well, maybe not so dangerous. Dogs always wander around at night.*

Sam stretched. *Why would Dracula bother some poor dog out sniffing the bushes?*

She rolled over to her other side. *He might be flying around Woodford right now.*

Sam stood up and shook herself. *That does it! I'm going to look.* She marched to the door and whined.

Joan looked up from her book. "Do you want to go out, Sam? You're restless tonight."

Sam whined again.

"All right," said Joan, "but don't go far."

She opened the door, and Sam stepped into the night.

12. A Narrow Escape

I'M TOO SMART TO GET CAUGHT!

As Sam trotted down the street, she noticed that Jennie's bedroom window was dark. *How can that kid sleep?*

Crossing the road, Sam entered the field and sniffed the air. In the moonlight, the pine trees whispered and swayed.

With a tiny growl, Sam moved toward the orchard. There she waited beside a fallen tree and listened. She sniffed again. Nothing.

She slipped through the fence hole — listening, sniffing, watching. She was alone with Dracula.

Sam inched around the corner of the house toward the front steps. She crouched in the weeds and looked around. There was something inside McIver's mailbox. She edged forward to get a better look. *He's probably got secret messages in there.* She craned her neck. *I wish I could see.* She jumped up and put her front paws on the mailbox.

CRASH! The mailbox post snapped in half and smashed to the ground! Sam went sprawling on top of it.

She tried to get up, but her paw was tangled in the wires that had held the old post together. She pulled her paw and shook it. *Oh no! I'm stuck!* Something rattled. She shook her paw harder. It rattled louder.

Suddenly Sam froze! She listened …

Click … Click … Click …

It was coming straight toward the door!

Sam yanked. Her paw came free. In a flash she bolted around the steps and flattened herself against the side of the house.

Click … Click … Click …

It's that sound again!

Click … Click …

Sam shivered. *I know what that sound is. It's his knees clicking! He's stiff from lying in his coffin all day!*

Click ... Click ...

The doorknob rattled and the door opened with the squeal of rusty hinges. "Go away!" shouted a voice.

It's Dracula!

Click ... Click ...

Footsteps were coming down the front steps. Any second, he'd turn the corner and see Sam.

She dove behind a bush and gulped back a growl. *I bet he's wearing his black cape. I bet he's got long fangs. I bet ...*

Click ... Click ...

"Go away!" shouted the voice again.

Click ... Click ...

Sam held her breath. Any second, she would see Dracula!

Suddenly the sound stopped. Sam's heart pounded. *He's changing into a bat!*

Silence. In her mind, Sam saw the fanged bat creature in Beth's book. She sniffed – the faint smell of soap came to her. *He's just washed his cape,* she thought with surprise.

Then there was nothing. Lightning bolts of fear crackled through Sam's body. She looked behind her. *If I run for my escape hole, he'll grab me.* She looked overhead for the bat and sniffed again. *I'm trapped behind this stupid bush.*

Click ... Click ... The sound grew fainter. *He's going back!*

Click ... Click ... Click ... The footsteps receded. Sam couldn't wait any longer. Crashing over the bush, she dashed for the back yard. Tripping and stumbling, she ran to the fence hole. She shoved herself through and raced out into the orchard.

Leaping over fallen branches, Sam ran across the moonlit field, across the road and up the street to her own door. She scratched at the door and barked.

The door opened immediately. "You bad dog!" cried Joan. "Where have you been?"

Sam slinked past Joan and hopped up on the spare bed. *Whew!* She shuddered. *Wait until*

Jennie and Beth hear about this.

Sam turned round and round and settled comfortably on the bed. Once her heart stopped pounding, she felt pleased with her bravery and cleverness. *Ha!* she thought smugly. *I'm too smart to get caught. Nothing to worry about. I can go there anytime I want.*

In fact, I think I'll go back first thing in the morning.

13. Sam's Great Idea

When Jennie rang the doorbell the next morning, Sam shoved against the door. Joan reached over her. "Get out of the way, Sam," she muttered.

Sam didn't move. "Hmph," muttered Joan. "Good morning, Jennie," she yawned.

"Hi, Joan. You look tired."

"I am tired," grumbled Joan. "Sam is in trouble today. She kept us up until midnight."

Jennie was surprised. "What happened?"

"She went out and we had to search for her for hours. Finally she came back."

Sam shoved past Jennie. *Let's get out of here. There's a big lecture coming.*

Joan watched coldly as Sam squeezed through the door and dashed down the walk.

"Uh, well. See you later, Joan." Jennie backed down the porch steps.

"Listen, Jennie," said Joan. "Be firm with Sam. She needs discipline."

Sam shot Jennie a nasty look. *Forget it. I don't allow discipline.*

Jennie led Sam to the corner of the back yard. "What have you done, Sam?"

Nothing bad. I just went over to McIver's to look around. And I lost track of time.

Jennie's hand flew to her mouth. "You went to McIver's alone?"

Yup.

"What happened?"

He came out of the house and I had to hide behind a bush.

"He came out of the house?"

Yup.

"Did he turn into a bat?"

I don't think he had time. He came out to see what the noise was.

"Noise? What noise?"

I knocked over the mailbox.

"Why did you knock over his mailbox?" Jennie squealed.

I was trying to see what was inside.

"Did you see his buggy eyes?"

I couldn't see him. When I was hiding, he came down the steps and yelled, "Go away!"

"What?" Jennie screeched.

He almost had me. If I wasn't so tough, I'd be in that coffin right now.

"You were nuts to go there."

I didn't think he'd bother a dog. Nobody bothers with dogs.

"I can't believe you did that."

I told you I was a great detective. Sam held her head up proudly. *I found out what makes the clicking sound.*

"What?"

His knees. I think they're stiff from lying in the coffin all day.

"We have to tell Beth." Jennie scrambled to her feet and led the way to Beth's house.

Beth couldn't believe it. "You mean Sam was that close to Dracula!"

Tell her I'm a great detective and I'm tough. And I need breakfast.

"Sam wants food."

Beth looked at Sam in amazement. "How can you eat? You did a very dangerous thing."

Sam ignored Beth. *Jennie, I want popcorn with ketchup.*

"I can't believe what this dog likes," muttered Beth when Jennie told her. She shoved popcorn into the microwave. "What do we do about McIver now?"

Jennie shrugged.

Sam gobbled popcorn. *Lucky I'm so smart. I'll think of something brilliant. Leave it to me.*

"Sam's going to think of something," Jennie said. "She's bragging about how smart she is."

Beth giggled.

Suddenly Sam jerked her head out of the bowl and stared at Jennie. *I've got it. We should deliver something!*

"You mean from the drugstore?" Jennie blinked.

Yup. You make the next delivery — instead of Noel.

"But Noel's making all the deliveries this summer. I agreed because I'm getting paid for walking you."

Tell him you want to do some deliveries too.

"I can't. We have an agreement. I'll do them when I'm older."

Well, unagree the agreement.

Jennie sighed. "Sam, a person can't just unagree something."

Hmph.

"Would you mind telling me what you two are talking about?" asked Beth.

"Sam thinks I should deliver something from the drugstore."

"That's a brilliant idea!" Beth patted Sam on the head. "You're very smart, Sam!"

Sam looked at Beth coldly. *Why is everyone always surprised?*

"Only one problem," said Jennie sadly. "Noel would never let us. He gets paid for each delivery."

Trick him.

"Sam thinks we should trick him."

Beth thought for a moment. "We'll call him and say he's won a contest and has to collect the prize."

"Noel wouldn't fall for that."

"We'll act like we're being really nice and doing him a favor," suggested Beth.

"That would never work." Jennie frowned.

Doesn't Noel have a girlfriend?

Jennie's face brightened. "Myrna!" she cried. "I'll give Noel a fake message that Myrna wants to meet him."

"Perfect!" Beth grinned.

"And I'll be a good sister and make the delivery so he can go."

"How will we know when something is going to be delivered to McIver?" asked Beth.

"Sam and I can go to the store every day and look in the delivery book."

And when we see McIver's name, Noel gets a message from Myrna. Very neat, very clever.

14. Spying on Dracula

A week passed. Jennie and Sam went to the drugstore every day, but McIver's name was never there.

One morning, Jennie sauntered over to the delivery book. There it was! McIver's name leaped off the page.

"Sam," she whispered, "today's the day!"

Sam wiggled her stubby tail. *Yahoo!*

"We'll wait for Noel outside."

Before long Noel roared up on his bike. "Hi, Jennie. I bet you want to help make deliveries, right?"

"Umm ... right."

Noel's eyes narrowed. "Why do you want to

help all of a sudden?"

"Because I'm nice," said Jennie. "And because Myrna called and wants you to go meet her."

Noel looked at Jennie closely. "So Myrna wants to go out and you just happen to be here. Is that it?"

"That's it. Quit being so suspicious, Noel."

Noel's face grew sly. "I'll only give you half my pay."

"I won't char – Oof!"

Sam nudged Jennie hard. *Charge him! Doing it for free will make him suspicious.*

Jennie folded her arms. "I want fifty cents a delivery."

"Dad gives me seventy-five cents. I pay half. That's thirty-seven cents. Take it or leave it."

"I'm charging fifty cents!" said Jennie stubbornly.

"And I'm paying thirty-seven cents," retorted Noel.

"And I'm charging fifty cents!" yelled Jennie.

Noel calmly turned his bike around. "I'll get Hugh Norton. He'll do it for thirty-seven cents."

Jennie sighed loudly. "Okay. Okay. I'll do it."

Noel grinned.

Jennie tried to look defeated. Sam chuckled quietly.

Noel stood up on his bike. "Have fun doing my deliveries for half price." As he wheeled around the corner, they heard him whistling a little tune.

Jennie giggled. "Noel thinks he's the smartest person in the world!"

He's wrong. I'm the smartest.

Minutes later, Jennie and Sam burst through Beth's gate with the parcels. "He's on the list today!" shouted Jennie.

Beth rushed to meet them. "How many deliveries do we have?" she asked.

"Six. We'll go to McIver's last."

"Let's do it," said Beth.

Grabbing their bikes, Jennie and Beth took off for the first delivery. They raced through the peaceful streets, leaving parcels at five houses. Then there was only one package left — McIver's.

"I'm scared." Standing with her bike, Jennie scuffed the dusty roadside with the toe of her sandals.

"Me too."

Sam looked up in disgust. *Don't get wimpy. We have to find his coffin.*

"W-we're safe in the daytime, aren't we?"

Beth nodded again. "People only got attacked at night."

"So we're all right?"

Beth nodded again.

"And Sam's good for protection too, isn't she?"

Quit worrying. I have wonderful teeth. As she ran beside the bikes, Sam pictured herself barking bravely at Dracula while Jennie and Beth huddled behind her. When the evil thing saw Sam, it screamed and flew up to the roof, gnashing its fangs …

Sam blinked and the dream disappeared.

They were on a quiet street in Woodford and Dracula was waiting. Only the squeaking of bikes and the soft padding of Sam's paws broke the still summer afternoon.

When they got to the end of the road, Beth felt that Dracula was very near. Jennie peered fearfully at the tall pines.

The dark house waited for them behind the trees. In silence, they went down the lane and climbed the steps to the front door. After a long minute, Beth reached up and knocked. The sound echoed.

The fur stood up on the back of Sam's neck. Beth knocked harder – this time, the door creaked open.

Sam, Jennie and Beth stared into the gloomy darkness.

15. Dracula's Victim

"Mr. McIver," called Beth. "It's the drugstore ... with your parcel."

Silence.

"Mr. McIver!" Beth called again.

Nothing moved. No one answered.

Beth leaned in the doorway and yelled as loudly as she could. "Mr. McIver!" The sound faded.

"What should we do?" she whispered.

Jennie looked at Sam.

He's asleep in his coffin. Let's take a quick look.

"Are you crazy?" Jennie whispered.

Not so crazy. How else are we going to see his coffin?

"What did Sam say?" asked Beth.

"She wants to go in, b-but it's dangerous."

Sam sat down firmly. *You two are wimps.*

"We are not!" Jennie hissed. "Beth, this dog is calling us wimps."

"That's a rotten thing to say, Sam," said Beth quietly. "We're just being careful." Beth leaned in the doorway and called into the gloom again. "Mr. McIver! It's the drugstore."

Silence.

"I want to find out if he's got a coffin, but …"

"We don't want to get trapped," finished Jennie. She looked pointedly at Sam. "Do we, Sam?"

Who's talking about getting trapped? I said a quick look.

"Only an idiot would go into Dracula's house," whispered Jennie.

So now I'm an idiot. I'm fed up with insults. Sam stood up, pushed the door open wider and marched into the gloom. *I'll let you two wimps know when I've found the coffin.*

Jennie and Beth gasped as Sam disappeared.

Inside the house, Sam tried to peer through the murky light. She listened. Not a sound. *My ears are perfect. There's nobody awake in here.*

She looked down the dim hallway — a coat rack, a chair, stairs and … *Yikes!* Sam looked straight into a pair of glassy eyes that were staring at her from high on the wall. She jumped. The eyes didn't move. Afraid to take her eyes off them, Sam slowly backed out the door.

Jennie and Beth were hanging on to each other as Sam edged out the door.

"What's the matter?" asked Jennie.

Sam's eyes were still glued on the glassy eyes.

Jennie shook Sam. "What is it?"

It's worse than we thought. He's got victims' heads on the wall.

Jennie gasped. "Beth, he's got heads on the wall!"

Beth caught her breath. "Count Dracula didn't cut up his victims."

Well, Count McIver does. Take a look.

16. Almost Trapped

Jennie tried to see into the darkness. "I can't see anything."

Go in a few steps.

Jennie looked anxiously at Beth. "Will you come with me?"

Beth nodded.

Together they stepped into the silent house. In the dim light, two enormous unblinking eyes stared at them from a far wall. Dead eyes.

Beth and Jennie grabbed each other. Sharp shivers of fear stabbed at them. Their fingertips tingled.

Suddenly Jennie giggled. "It's a deer head."

Beth looked more closely. Jennie was right.

Beth went back outside. "It's a deer head," she told Sam quietly.

So?

"So?" giggled Jennie as she stepped out the door. "So it's not a victim."

What do you mean, not a victim?

"It's only an animal," laughed Jennie.

Sam stared at her.

Jennie's smile crumpled. "Oh. I – I – I didn't mean that, Sam. I mean, I didn't mean it the way it sounded."

Sam stared.

Jennie stumbled on. "Uh … What I mean is … it's sort of normal to hang a deer head on your wall."

Sam snorted. *Normal! Ask the deer if he thinks it's so normal.*

"Okay, maybe not normal, but a lot of people do it."

Hmph. I'm going in again. She stepped into the gloomy hall.

"We can't let Sam go alone," said Beth, tugging at Jennie's arm. "And we don't want her calling us wimps."

Taking a deep breath, the girls stepped into the stillness.

Sam looked back at them. *About time.*

"It's the drugstore, Mr. McIver!" shouted Beth. But there was no answer.

No one's here ... The place is empty ... except the basement, of course.

Sam moved down the hallway, and Jennie and Beth followed. The floor creaked. Every step made them wince.

Computer parts and dirty dishes littered the kitchen. From the ceiling, a lightbulb dangled on a frayed cord. The silence of the house wrapped itself around them.

Sam sniffed at a bolted door. *This is the basement!*

Both girls froze.

They all stared at the door. "Sam says it's the basement," mouthed Jennie.

Open it! We'll never find the coffin unless we look.

Jennie gulped and looked at Beth. With shaking hands, Beth slid back the bolt. Gripping the cracked knob, she opened the door. The hinges shrieked.

The basement lay below them like a tomb. Rickety stairs led down into the moldy damp, down into the unknown.

Sam stepped on the stairs. *Come on, you wimps.*

Slowly, Jennie and Beth followed.

In the murky light, they could see the rough stone walls, the damp brick floor and dusty windows covered in cobwebs. An octopus-like furnace stood in the center of the cellar, its tentacles reaching through the ceiling. Everywhere were boxes, boards, trunks and piles of newspapers.

Jennie tugged on Beth's sleeve. "Do you see a coffin?" Beth shook her head.

Sam sniffed at the boxes. Jennie and Beth stayed close behind. "Hurry up, Sam," hissed Jennie. "One more minute and we're out of here."

As Sam nosed around the cellar, beetles scuttled away and cobwebs filled her nose. *No coffin here.* Then she caught her breath. *Wait a minute! Behind those boxes is a door!*

With their hearts thudding, Jennie and Beth moved some boxes. Sam threw her weight against the door. It swung open and cold air washed over them. Light filtered through tiny slatted windows and striped across shelves of dusty jars.

There was nothing in the room.

"Let's get out of here," said Jennie.

But as they started back to the stairs, they heard a noise. Terror flashed through their bodies.

The front door had banged shut.

Footsteps thumped down the hallway. Thud ... Thud ... Thud ... Click ... Click ... Click ... Someone went into the kitchen.

"Who left my front door open!" bellowed a voice.

Jennie and Beth froze in their tracks.

The basement door slammed and the bolt clicked.

"We're trapped!" Beth's face was white against her bright red hair.

A window! cried Sam. *Climb out a window and run!*

"Who's been in here?" muttered the voice. Click … Click … Click …

Quick!

Jennie clambered onto a trunk and pulled at a dusty window. She and Beth yanked it open and scrambled out. Sam stood on her hind legs and clawed at the stone wall. The girls reached down and grabbed Sam. Sam scrambled with her back legs while the girls pulled on her front legs. Scraping her stomach, Sam squeezed out the window.

In a flash, they streaked across the back of the house and through the fence hole into the orchard.

Rolling over and over in the grass, Sam kicked her feet in the air to get rid of any crawly things stuck in her fur. Then she walked over to the girls and slurped at their faces. *Thanks, I owe you a big one.*

Jennie gave Sam a hug and Beth threw her arms around Sam's neck. Sam soaked Beth's curly hair with her slobbery tongue.

Then Sam stood up and stared at Jennie. *Enough celebrating already. I'm starving.*

Jennie laughed. "You can eat all the junk you want, Sam. I won't nag you. I promise."

You mean it?

"Of course I mean it."

Good. I want smoky bacon chips with pistachio ice cream and ketchup.

17. Something's Wrong

Later that night, the three friends lounged on Jennie's bed. Sam drank cream soda out of a bowl. Smacking her chops, she grabbed her fourth piece of red licorice and belched.

"If you throw up, Sam, you're cleaning up the mess," said Jennie through a mouthful of peanuts.

Dogs don't clean up. Sam lapped up some peanuts. *I have to eat to calm my nerves.*

Jennie sighed. "Sam says she's calming her nerves."

Beth giggled.

"We were really stupid to go in there. Weren't we, Sam?" Jennie looked pointedly at Sam.

How else would we find his coffin?

"But we didn't find it," said Jennie.

"Something's wrong." Beth furrowed her brow and chewed a fingernail. "We should have found a coffin."

Sam looked up from the chips she was crunching. *Yeah. So where does he keep it?*

"And he shouldn't be walking around during the day. He should be sleeping." Beth scratched her head.

Just then, Noel poked his head in the door. "Myrna wasn't there to meet me, little sister."

Jennie changed the subject quickly. "Noel," she said sweetly, "do you know anything about Dracula?"

"Sure. Everybody does."

"He sleeps in a coffin in the basement. Right?"

"Right."

"Is it always in the basement?"

"Who knows?" Noel looked at them strangely. "Why do you care?"

"Because," Jennie paused dramatically, "we

think we've found him."

Noel looked puzzled. "You can't find him. He's not real."

"Yes he is," said Beth firmly. "We read a classic comic about him."

Amazement spread over Noel's face. "Wow, you kids are dumb. Dracula's a story. Somebody made it up."

"You mean Count Dracula never lived in Transylvania?" Beth squinted at Noel.

"Of course not." Noel looked at them through narrow eyes. "So, exactly who is supposed to be Dracula?"

"Weird old McIver," blurted Beth.

Noel began to laugh. He laughed so hard he had to hold on to his stomach. "You two are nuts!"

Jennie, Beth and Sam sat in stony silence.

"You actually thought Mr. McIver was Dracula!" Noel gasped.

Beth and Jennie glared.

Sam sniffed. *Is something funny here?*

"Forget we said that, Noel," muttered Jennie.

But Noel was not going to forget it. He collapsed on the bed, wiping tears of laughter from his eyes.

Sam moved away and eyed Noel with distaste. *Did somebody say you could sit near me?*

"Who said you could sit on my bed?" asked Jennie coldly.

Noel ignored her. "What gave you the idea McIver was Dracula? He's a recluse, you idiots!"

Jennie decided not to ask what a recluse was. She stared at the wallpaper as if it was fascinating.

Beth blushed to the roots of her hair. She couldn't stand being laughed at.

Noel had to be wrong.

18. One Last Chance

"Noel's wrong." Beth yanked a sweater furiously over her curls. "I'm going to the library. It's open until eight o'clock."

Jennie and Sam waited impatiently for Beth to come back. "Of course Noel's wrong," muttered Jennie. "He's always wrong."

I hate teenagers. Have I ever told you that?

When Beth burst back into the bedroom, she threw a book on the bed. "Mrs. Oates gave me this book of facts. She says Count Dracula really lived, but he wasn't a vampire."

Jennie sat up. "What else did she say?"

Sadly, Beth flopped on the bed. "She said vampires aren't real. Dracula's made up. He's just in a novel."

I told you reading was a waste of time.

Jennie looked disappointed. "A novel's just a made-up story, isn't it?"

Beth flipped glumly through the book of facts. "I bet Noel was right."

Sam slurped a long string of licorice. *Teenagers are never right. They're big pimply-faced know-it-all oafs.*

Beth looked up from the page she was reading. "It's true!" she cried. "There are no vampires!"

"Do you think Noel was right about Mr. McIver being a recluse?" Jennie sadly twirled a strand of her hair.

What would a big spiky-haired teenage oaf know about that?

Jennie grabbed the dictionary her Aunt Ada had given her for Christmas. She flipped the pages to "R" and read, "Recluse — one who chooses to live alone." She threw the dictionary on the floor.

Sam looked up from the empty peanut bowl. *Why would his knees click?*

Jennie shrugged. "I don't know why his knees click. I wish I did."

His knees click because he's a vampire.

"There are no vampires. It says so, right here in this book, Sam."

Why should I believe some book?

"Because it's a book of facts," Jennie insisted.

Beth slumped against the wall. "We shouldn't have believed that Dracula story. It didn't say it was true. I just thought it was true."

Sam flopped on the pillows. *So Dracula doesn't live in Woodford after all. Phooey.*

Jennie stared at the ceiling. "If McIver's not Dracula, then what is he?"

Beth slouched farther down the wall. "He must be a criminal — like you thought at first."

Who wants to spy on a crummy ordinary crook?

Sam slumped on the bed. She was about to say she needed a new mystery when the idea of a criminal took hold in her mind. She saw herself catching McIver, the world-famous robber. People were gathered at the police station to see the wonder dog. Sam stood on the steps of the station and bowed to the cheering crowd ...

"We have to find out the truth." Beth gritted her teeth. "Or Noel will laugh at us forever."

"Maybe we should just forget it," said Jennie with a sinking heart. "We can ignore Noel."

I refuse to be laughed at by a pimply faced oaf.

"Never." Beth thought about their detective list. "No more messing around. We'll interview McIver," she muttered.

Sam jumped up and put her paw in the bowl of cream soda. *Yeah! We'll say we're with the police and I'm a police dog. And we know he's a crook and we demand to know what's going on.*

Jennie looked nervously at Sam. "We are not going to say any of that stuff, Sam. We have to be careful."

Sam sniffed. *Okay. Okay.* Then she groaned as a sharp pain knotted her stomach. *Those peanuts must have been rotten.*

But Jennie wasn't listening.

"We'd better plan this interview carefully," Beth said grimly. "It's our last chance."

19. A Surprising Interview

By noon the next day, they were ready. They were going to say it was a summer project for school and their teacher had asked them to find out why people chose to move to Woodford.

"He's probably going to tell us to get lost," Jennie worried.

"Maybe not. If he's hiding, he won't want people to be suspicious."

Jennie chewed her lip. "Do you think this is dangerous?"

Relax. Did I ever tell you I have wonderful teeth?

"Noel teased me about Woodford's vampire all morning," said Jennie. "I can't stand it."

"Let's go then," Beth gathered clipboards, pencils and paper.

Ten minutes later, they were at McIver's place. The front steps creaked as they went up to the porch. Beth took a deep breath and knocked. At first there was no answer. She knocked again.

"Who is it?" growled a voice.

"It's Jennie Levinsky and Beth Morrison," called Beth.

"Go away. I don't know Jennie Levinsky or Beth Morrison."

"M-may we talk to you for a minute, s-sir?" squeaked Jennie.

No answer came through the door. An eerie silence hung over the porch.

Come on, you guys. Make him talk.

"Sure, Sam," whispered Jennie. "We'll order him to open up."

Beth knocked again.

"Stop banging on my door!" shouted the voice.

"Our teacher asked us to talk to people," said Beth firmly.

"Tell your teacher I hate kids."

Sam cocked her head as she heard the clicking. The sound was getting louder. It was moving toward the door. Click ... Click ... Click ...

The doorknob turned, first one way, then the other. A chain rattled and the door opened a crack. "Talk fast," said the voice.

Beth cleared her throat. "Excuse us for bothering you, Mr. McIver. We're doing a project for school on why people choose to live in Woodford ..." Her voice trailed off.

"I'm busy."

You have a lovely personality.

"It's for school, sir."

They waited. Click ... Click ... Click ... "I'll talk to you for exactly one minute. No more."

Don't smother us with charm.

With a squeak the door opened wider. Before them stood Mr. McIver.

Well! If it isn't old buggy bat eyes himself.

Mr. McIver was huge and wild looking. He wore green coveralls and held a computer circuit board in one hand. Bulging light blue eyes stared at them through thick, thick glasses. His scowl was framed by a halo of electric hair.

The girls stepped back.

Mr. McIver leaned toward them. His eyes got bigger and buggier. "Time is running out."

Jennie and Beth swallowed.

Sam looked closely at him. *I can't decide if those are insect eyes or bat eyes.* She sniffed. The ordinary smells of shampoo and soap wafted into her nose. *He doesn't smell like a bug or a bat.*

"I'm not going to stand here all day," Mr. McIver muttered. His hair shook when he talked.

Just then, Sam did a surprising thing. She went up to Mr. McIver and nuzzled his hand. Mr. McIver smiled.

Jennie jumped with alarm. "Sam! Come here!" Sam ignored her and rubbed against Mr. McIver's leg.

Mr. McIver smiled again. "Pleased to meet you, Sam. I like dogs a lot better than I like people."

Sam chuckled and held up her paw. *Very wise. You have excellent taste.*

"Do you want to know why I moved to Woodford?" boomed Mr. McIver, turning his huge eyes back to Jennie and Beth.

The girls gulped and nodded.

"I moved to Woodford," he said, "so nobody would bother me!" And he slammed the door.

20. McIver's Secret

Sam couldn't stop thinking about McIver. *He's not a bug or a bat person. If he was, I'd smell it. He's a regular human, but something is different. Hmm ... What could a strange guy like that be hiding?*

Maybe he has somebody trapped in the attic. No ... I'd be able to smell another person. Maybe he's got gold buried in the yard. Tingles raced down Sam's spine, and her mind whirred. *I bet he was a bank robber in the old days ... Maybe he was supposed to be hanged but he escaped ... Maybe he came to Woodford to hide ... Wonderful.*

That evening Sam wandered through the yard to Jennie's back porch. "Hi, Sam." Jennie's voice came out of the darkness.

Sam went over to the steps and laid her chin on Jennie's knee. *So, what do you think McIver's secret is?*

"We know McIver's secret. He's a weird recluse who hates kids."

He needs a reason to be a recluse.

"He doesn't need a reason. And if he does have a reason, I don't care what it is. Noel is laughing like a hyena about Dracula. I'm not going to be caught with any more crazy ideas."

It wasn't a crazy idea. We were a bit wrong, that's all.

Jennie snorted. "We were a lot wrong."

Phooey. That happens in the detective business.

"Forget the detective business."

Sam looked up sharply. *Don't you care about McIver anymore?*

"Nope." Jennie was firm.

Sam felt her heart sink. *But Beth cares, doesn't she?*

"Nope." Jennie sounded even firmer.

Well ... Beth probably wants a new mystery.

Jennie shook her head. "No, she doesn't."

Sam was getting cranky. *You two are boring. One minute we have Dracula right here in Woodford and we're having a great time. The next minute nobody cares.*

Just then, Jennie's mother called her to come in. "See you tomorrow, Sam," whispered Jennie. "I'm sorry there's no mystery, but Beth and I don't want to look stupid anymore."

So who cares about looking stupid? It's the adventure that matters.

Sadly, Sam watched Jennie go in. Then she padded silently between the houses to the street. *Who says there's no mystery? I think I'll take a stroll over to McIver's.*

Sam marched through the dark streets, across the road, through the field, into the old orchard and through the fence hole. She went around the house straight to McIver's front door. She barked. A light went on.

"Woof! Woof!" Sam barked again. The door opened a crack.

McIver's round glasses, huge eyes and wild

hair peered around the door. "Well, well," he boomed. "If it isn't Sam!"

When he opened the door wide, Sam jumped on him. McIver patted her. Then he looked down the lane. "You haven't brought those horrible kids, have you?"

Sam chuckled to herself. "Woof!"

"All alone, huh? Good. You can come in."

Sam stepped into the dim hall and trotted past the deer head toward the kitchen. *Let's see if weird guys give snacks.* Suddenly she stopped and cocked her head. Click ... Click ... She looked questioningly at McIver. "Woof!"

McIver's big bug eyes crinkled behind his thick glasses. "Meet Joe," he chuckled as a tiny robot glided around the corner into the hall, its lights flashing and small antennae waving.

"Woof!" Sam backed up nervously.

Joe glided toward her.

This thing looks like an insect. Maybe it's his son.

Joe's clicking got louder and louder. Click ... Click ...

"I made Joe last year," explained McIver. "Okay, Joe, you can stop now," he said when the robot got to Sam's feet.

"Bleep," said Joe. His lights flashed. "Bleep. Bleep."

Sam backed up some more. "Woof! Woof! Woof!"

"Bleep," said Joe.

Bleep yourself. Don't touch my toes or I'll chomp off your antennae.

McIver laughed, and his wild hair shook. "Joe won't hurt you. He's my best friend. I trust him because he's not a person. I learned long ago that you can't trust people."

All the same, watch the toes.

McIver led the way to the kitchen. "Come on, Joe. This way."

"Bleep. Bleep." Joe turned around and clicked his way into the kitchen.

Sam watched Joe go down the hall. *There's the mystery of the clicking. Wait until I tell Jennie.*

McIver kept talking. "I just finished my new snack machine Sam. Come and try it."

Sam's head perked up. *Did this guy say "snack machine"?*

Dirty dishes and tools still littered the kitchen counter. On the table was the wooden box filled with equipment. In the middle of the floor was the most interesting machine Sam had ever seen. McIver pushed a button and the whole thing started to whir.

Sam watched in amazement as snacks slid down slides, through loops, down funnels and round and round until they popped out the other end of the machine. The first thing to pop out was a green cookie. Sam sniffed.

"Go ahead. Try it," chortled McIver. He beamed at Sam with his huge eyes. "My machine makes forty-seven different snacks!"

Sam nibbled. *Peppermint!* She gobbled it up and smacked her chops.

"What would you like next?" asked McIver. From his green coveralls he pulled out a small black flashlight. He stuck it between his teeth and shone the light on the control panel. He squinted at the writing. "I have terrible eyesight," he explained, "that's why I wear these thick glasses and need this light."

There's the mystery of the light shining out of an insect mouth!

Leaning very close to the control panel, McIver read, "Chocolate ice cream blobbies, chocolate nut clusters, butterscotch dreams, raspberry delights —"

"Woof!" barked Sam.

"Raspberry delights it is," cried McIver, his hair waving with excitement. "Here it comes!" He flipped a switch and the machine came alive again. Whir. Click. Bing. Pop! Little red blobs rolled down the slides, through the funnels and into the dish. Plop. Plop. Plop.

Sam lapped them up. They were smoother and creamier and more delicious than any candy she had ever tasted. "Woof!"

"How about a pistachio crunchie?" asked McIver, flapping his arms crazily. He flipped the switch again. Sam licked up pistachio crunchies as fast as they popped out.

She belched cheerfully. *I love this guy.*

Sam sat in the kitchen and watched. While McIver worked on the machine, he shone the flashlight from his mouth and hummed a mournful, moaning song. Joe clicked his way around the kitchen and bleeped at Sam as he went past. Every few minutes, McIver jumped up and flipped a switch, and a wonderful snack plopped into the dish.

After two hours, the room started to spin. *Aaghh!* Sam thought as she lay down blearily. *Maybe I ate too much.*

But McIver didn't notice. He just kept talking and humming and bringing out his inventions. He had a sunshine machine to carry around on rainy days. He had a remote-control butterfly that spied on suspicious people. He had a paintbox that never ran out.

Wait until Jennie and Beth see this!

"... I don't want to meet your friends, Sam," McIver was saying. "At least, not yet."

Sam looked up in surprise.

"My first invention was stolen and I've never trusted people since." He beamed at

Sam through his thick glasses. "I trust you because you're a dog, and I trust Joe because he's a robot."

"Bleep," said Joe happily and clicked his way over to McIver.

When Sam went outside and walked down the drive, she noticed how dark everything was. Set behind tall pines in a lonely field, the house could hardly be seen. There was only one dim light in the kitchen. *I see now why nobody sees lights on.* Sam saw the movement of McIver's flashlight. *That's the moving light.*

As she trotted along, Sam chuckled. McIver's mournful song drifted through the open windows. *There's the moaning.*

I have all the answers now. I know what the clicking is. I know why he's a recluse. I know why he has buggy, bat eyes. It's just his thick glasses that make his eyes look that way. Sam turned onto her own street and padded past Jennie's dark window. *Wait until you hear all this, Jennie.*

Later as she settled down on the spare bed, Sam thought about the friendly way Joe had bleeped at her when she left. "Come again, Sam," McIver had called.

You can bet on it, she thought as she stretched out. *What a great place.* She sighed happily.

As Sam drifted off to sleep, she let her mind wander to all her favorite things — witches, goblins, monsters, giants. *Nothing like a good mystery,* she thought, snuggling deeper into the pillows.

Suddenly her head jerked up. *Mystery! I don't have a mystery! I just solved it!*

A panicky feeling started to grow inside Sam. *Life without adventure is boring ... And boredom is bad ... Very bad.*

I've got to find another mystery right away.

But Sam was very tired. She lay her head down sleepily ...

Jennie and I can start looking first thing in the morning ...